THE SETTLEMENT OF NEW FRANCE AND ACADIA
1524-1701

TITLE LIST

THE SETTLEMENT OF NEW FRANCE AND ACADIA
1524-1701

BY
SHEILA NELSON

MASON CREST PUBLISHERS
PHILADELPHIA

Mason Crest Publishers Inc.
370 Reed Road
Broomall, Pennsylvania 19008
(866) MCP-BOOK (toll free)

First printing
1 2 3 4 5 6 7 8 9 10

Library of Congress Cataloging-in-Publication Data

Nelson, Sheila.
   The settlement of New France and Acadia, 1524–1701 / by Sheila Nelson.
      v. cm. — (How Canada became Canada)
   Includes index.
   Contents: France in the new world — First colonies of New France — The province of Canada — Acadia — The royal province — Wars and conflicts in New France.
   ISBN 1-4222-0002-7   ISBN 1-4222-0000-0 (series)
   1. Canada—History—To 1763 (New France)—Juvenile literature. 2. Frontier and pioneer life—Canada—Juvenile literature. 3. Land settlement—Canada—History—Juvenile literature. 4. Acadia—History—Juvenile literature. I. Title.
   F1030.N324 2005
   971.01—dc22
                                  2005004468

Produced by Harding House Publishing Service, Inc.
www.hardinghousepages.com
Interior design by MK Bassett-Harvey.
Cover design by Dianne Hodack.
Printed in the Hashemite Kingdom of Jordan.

CONTENTS

INTRODUCTION

by David Bercuson

Every country's history is distinct, and so is Canada's. Although Canada is often said to be a pale imitation of the United States, it has a unique history that has created a modern North American nation on its own path to democracy and social justice. This series explains how that happened.

Canada's history is rooted in its climate, its geography, and in its separate political development. Virtually all of Canada experiences long, dark, and very cold winters with copious amounts of snowfall. Canada also spans several distinct geographic regions, from the rugged western mountain ranges on the Pacific coast to the forested lowlands of the St. Lawrence River Valley and the Atlantic tidewater region.

Canada's regional divisions were complicated by the British conquest of New France at the end of the Seven Years' War in 1763. Although Britain defeated France, the French were far more numerous in Canada than the British. Britain was thus forced to recognize French Canadian rights to their own language, religion, and culture. That recognition is now enshrined in the Canadian Constitution. It has made Canada a democracy that values group rights alongside individual rights, with official French/English bilingualism as a key part of the Canadian character.

During the American Revolution, Canadians chose to stay British. After the Revolution, they provided refuge to tens of thousands of Americans who, for one reason or another, did not follow George Washington, Benjamin Franklin, or the other founders of the United States who broke with Britain.

Democracy in Canada under the British Crown evolved more slowly than it did in the United States. But in the early nineteenth century, slavery was outlawed in the

British Empire, and as a result, also in Canada. Thus Canada never experienced civil war or government-imposed racial segregation.

From these few, brief examples, it is clear that Canada's history differs considerably from that of the United States. And yet today, Canada is a true North American democracy in its own right. Canadians will profit from a better understanding of how their country was shaped—and Americans may learn much about their own country by studying the story of Canada.

France's early voyages to the New World

One

FRANCE IN THE NEW WORLD

As he sat aboard his ship the *Dauphine* on July 8, 1524, Giovanni da Verrazano thought back on his voyage to the recently discovered western lands. Soon, he would be in France. Before he arrived, he needed to write an account of his journeys to send to King Francis I. He thought for a moment and then wrote,

> Since the storm that we encountered in the northern regions, Most Serene King, I have not written to tell Your Majesty of what happened to the four ships which you sent over the Ocean to explore new lands, as I thought that you had already been informed of everything—how we were forced by the fury of the winds to return in distress to Brittany with only the *Normandy* and the *Dauphine*, and that after undergoing repairs there, began our voyage with these two ships, equipped for war, following the coasts of Spain, Your Most Serene Majesty will have heard; and then according to our new plan, we continued the original voyage with only the *Dauphine*; now on our return from this voyage I will tell Your Majesty of what we found.

France's King Francis had hired Verrazano, an Italian navigator, to explore the new lands discovered across the Atlantic Ocean, claiming them for France and looking for a Northwest Passage—a way to sail ships through them to the Pacific Ocean and beyond to Asia. Verrazano's 1524 voyage was the first recorded French expedition to travel to the New World.

Verrazano set sail from the island of Madeira, off the coast of Portugal, on January 17, 1524. On around March 1, his ship reached the coast of North America, near Cape Fear, North Carolina. Over the next several months, Verrazano traveled up the coast, meeting the native people of the area (and kidnapping one young boy) before returning to France to make his report.

Giovanni da Verrazano

Jacques Cartier Comes to Canada

Ten years after Verrazano's voyage, King Francis decided to send out another expedition. This expedition would also look for the Northwest Passage leading through North America to the Pacific Ocean, but this time the explorers would search out the riches of the New World as well. Jacques Cartier, from St. Malo in northern France, led the expedition.

Cartier left France on April 20, 1534, arriving in Newfoundland on May 10. He sailed north around Newfoundland's Northern Peninsula and then south through

He named the east coast of North America Acadia after the beautiful, mythical land of Arcadia from Greek legend.

Verrazano concluded that this "obstacle of new land" lay between Europe and Asia, a much larger land than had first been thought. This land, Verrazano wrote to the French king, "appears to be larger than our Europe, than Africa, and almost larger than Asia, if we estimate its size correctly."

A fifteenth-century explorer's ship

the Strait of Belle Isle between Labrador and Newfoundland, proving finally that Newfoundland was actually an island. With its barren rock and thin, sparse soil, the landscape of Labrador did not impress him; he described it as "the land God gave to Cain" and sailed on, hoping the rest of this New World would be more promising. In the Gulf of St. Lawrence, Cartier was relieved to discover the flat and fertile Prince Edward Island, calling it "the fairest land 'tis possible to see."

Along the coast of New Brunswick, Cartier encountered a large group of Mi'kmaq, eager to trade for European goods. As the French explored the coastline in a longboat, the Mi'kmaq approached them in forty canoes, motioning happily to the Europeans. The sight of so many native people alarmed the French, and they motioned the Mi'kmaq to stay away. When the Mi'kmaq kept coming, Cartier shot two small cannons over their heads. The Mi'kmaq turned away immediately and left.

On the Gaspé Peninsula, Cartier met a group of Iroquoian who had traveled down the St. Lawrence from their village Stadacona on a summer fishing trip. The **First Nations** group at first greeted the French warmly and held a celebration of feasting and dancing. Afterward, Cartier set up a huge wooden cross, carved with the words, "Long Live the King of France." This cross made many of the Iroquoians nervous and angry. They believed Cartier was trying to lay claim to their land, and their leader, Donnacona, furiously gestured to the cross, the land around, and himself, meaning the French should not have set up the cross without his permission.

To calm Donnacona, Cartier invited him and his two sons, Domagaya and Taignoagny, aboard the French ship to trade. On the ship, Cartier had Domagaya and Taignoagny dressed up in shirts, red caps, and brass chains—which they

First Nations is the term used to describe the Native people of Canada.

Jacques Cartier

Cartier's cross

enjoyed—and asked Donnacona to let his sons travel back to France with him. Donnacona gave his permission, said good-bye to his sons, and watched as the French ship sailed away.

The Second Voyage

In France, Domagaya and Taignoagny learned French and told Cartier about a fan-tastic place called Saguenay, filled with gold and other treasure. They also told him about the St. Lawrence River, the wide waterway cutting into the interior of the continent. No one had followed the river to its end, they said, and Cartier immediately thought of the Northwest Passage leading across the New World to Asia.

In 1535, Cartier agreed to return to the New World and take Domagaya and Taignoagny with him. Their stories about the riches of Saguenay and the thought of a possible Northwest Passage had finally convinced him to go back.

The two young Iroquoians guided Cartier up the St. Lawrence to their home village of Stadacona (the future site of Québec City). Donnacona was overjoyed to see his sons again and hugged them tightly. The village celebrated the return of the chief's sons, and many of the Iroquoians were friendly with the French. Domagaya and Taignoagny, however, refused to go near the French ship. Now that they were home, they did not want to risk being taken away again.

As Domagaya and Taignoagny became less friendly, Cartier started to distrust them. He worried they were not translating accurately as they spoke with their father on his behalf. Earlier, Taignoagny had agreed to take the French further upriver to the village of Hochelaga. Now, he changed his mind and claimed the trip was not worthwhile. This made Cartier want to go to Hochelaga even more, because he now thought Taignoagny was trying to hide something from him.

Donnacona and his sons feared the French wanted to take over their land, so they tried to keep them from traveling through any more of the region. Donnacona warned Cartier that winter would soon come, trapping the French upriver. Cartier

The Naming of Canada

As Domagaya and Taignoagny neared Stadacona, they spoke of *kanata*. Cartier understood them to mean *kanata* was the name of the land around them and named the country Canada. Actually, Domagaya and Taignoagny meant "the village," which is what *kanata* means. For years, the French called the area along the St. Lawrence River Canada. The region was one of the provinces of New France—the French land in the New World. Acadia was another province. Later, people started calling the whole country Canada.

SHIPS OF THE TIME OF CABOT AND CARTIER

The Grand Hermine, Cartier's largest ship of 126 tons.

End of the 15th Century.

was not bothered by thoughts of snow and ice; the weather was warm, and autumn had barely begun.

In late September, Cartier and his men set out from Stadacona upriver toward Hochelaga (the present site of Montréal), taking Domagaya and Taignoagny with them. The First Nations people at Hochelaga greeted them warmly, but Cartier had no success finding his Northwest Passage; just upriver from Hochelaga, the river became impassable with shallow rapids.

By the time Cartier left Hochelaga, Donnacona's predictions had come true and the river had begun to freeze. The French made it back to Stadacona, where they quickly built a fort to spend the winter. Donnacona did not like the French staying near his village, but he liked even less the fact that they kept cannons on the walls of their fort, pointed out at the Iroquoians.

Cartier and his men suffered through a long, hard winter, and the Iroquoians did not have a much better time. Disease broke out among the Native people—likely

Cartier with the Iroquoians

brought by the French; at least fifty Iroquoians died over the winter. When the French began to get sick, Cartier assumed they had caught the disease from the Iroquoians. Cartier's men, however, had developed scurvy, a condition caused by too little vitamin C.

Some of the Native people—including Domagaya—suffered from scurvy as well. When Cartier saw Domagaya one day, though, he looked perfectly healthy, even though he had been very sick not long before. Surprised, Cartier asked Domagaya what had cured him. The young man showed Cartier how he had made a tea from the leaves of a white cedar, which had cured him.

Cartier did not trust Domagaya and thought he might be trying to poison him by getting him to drink the white cedar tea. Some of the French sailors were so sick, though, they were willing to try anything; they eagerly drank the tea and immediately felt much better. When the other French saw the effect the tea had on their friends, they all wanted to try the tea. Eight days later, the white cedar tree near the French fort had been stripped bare and everyone felt much better. Unfortunately, the French did not discover the cure for scurvy until

March, after twenty-five men had already died.

When spring came, Cartier wanted to return to France. He also wanted to take Donnacona with him. Donnacona did not trust the French, and Cartier could not convince the Iroquoian chief to come with him willingly—so he kidnapped him, along with his two sons, and took them back to the ship. When Cartier left for France, he took ten Iroquoians with

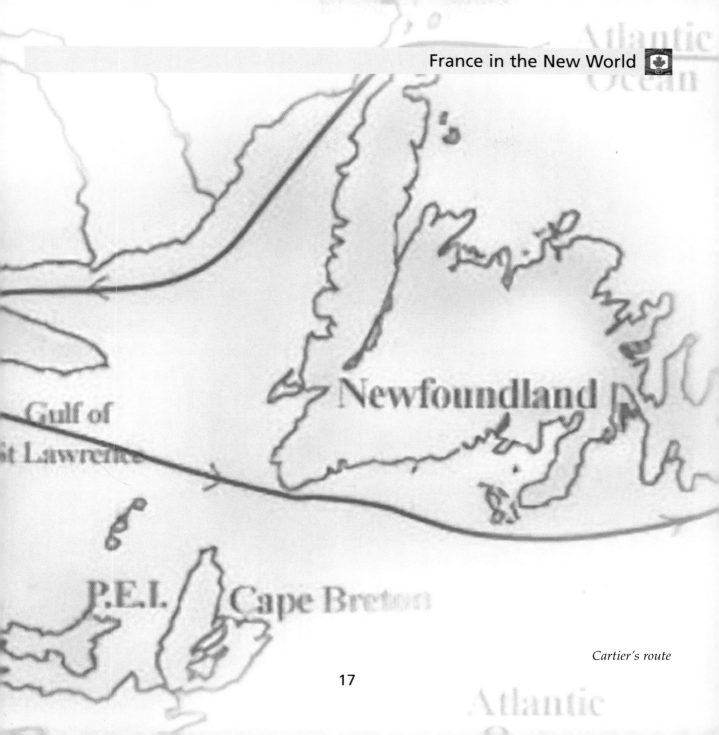

Atlantic Ocean

Gulf of
St Lawrence

Newfoundland

P.E.I. Cape Breton

Atlantic

Cartier's route

17

Cartier paved the way for the settlers who came to Newfoundland's rocky coast.

him—Donnacona, Domagaya, Taignoagny, three other men, and four children. None of these First Nations people ever returned to Canada, and only one little girl lived for very long in Europe.

Cartier's Last Voyage to Canada

In 1541, Cartier went back to Canada one last time. He had almost given up on finding the Northwest Passage in the St. Lawrence, but he could not forget the stories he had heard about Saguenay. He doubted everything the Iroquoians had told him about Saguenay was true—spices could never grow in the cool Canadian climate, for example—but if even some of the stories of gold and riches had been accurate, Cartier wanted to find the mythical kingdom.

This time, however, none of the Iroquoians along the St. Lawrence were friendly to Cartier. The people of Stadacona especially mistrusted him. He had taken their chief and others from their village— and he had not brought them back as he had promised.

Cartier tried to start up a small colony along the banks of the St. Lawrence, but problems instantly arose. Warriors from Stadacona attacked the settlement, killing thirty-five colonists. The weather was terrible. And no one had seen any sign of Saguenay, and nobody knew if it really existed.

Cartier had had enough. He gathered up as much as he could of what he thought might be gold and diamonds and headed back to France. It was the last straw when he discovered that instead of gold and diamonds, he had really carried home iron pyrite—often called fool's gold—and quartz rocks.

Cartier had not accomplished any of his goals in the seven years he had spent making voyages to Canada and exploring the St. Lawrence region. He had neither found a trade passage to Asia nor discovered great wealth in the New World. Nevertheless, Cartier had paved the way for future explorers and settlers in Canada. He had explored and charted the area around the St. Lawrence River, and most important, he had familiarized the French people with Canada.

An early map of France's colonies in the New World

FIRST COLONIES OF NEW FRANCE

Back in the autumn of 1604, the tiny island had looked like the perfect place for a colony. Nestled in the middle of the St. Croix River, several miles inland from Passamaquoddy Bay, the French had thought the island would make a good settlement, easily defended from First Nations tribes on the mainland. They cut down nearly all the trees on the little island and used them to build houses for the seventy-nine men of the colony, and to surround the settlement with a wall for defense. Pierre du Gua de Monts, who governed the colony, expected to send out hunting parties throughout the winter to bring back firewood and fresh meat.

On October 6, snow began to fall. By early December, the river was clogged with huge chunks of ice, stranding the French on the island. A band of Maliseet watched from the shore, and de Monts worried they planned to attack. Soon, the colonists started to get sick. Their gums bled and their joints ached. Through the long winter, they huddled together for warmth, chewing the salted meats they had brought with them and melting snow for drinking water. They rationed out the rest of the trees to feed their small fires over the next several months. By May, when the last of the ice finally cleared the river, thirty-five men had died of scurvy, and another twenty lay at death's door.

*A **trade monopoly** is the complete control of trade by one company or organization.*

St. Croix Island

For the last half of the sixteenth century, France had been too absorbed with problems at home to sponsor any official expeditions to the New World. Since Jacques Cartier left Canada in 1542, the only Frenchmen in North America had been independent fur trappers and fishermen. In France, the Wars of Religion raged from 1562 to 1598. Fought between the Roman Catholics and the Huguenots (French Protestants), the war was brought on by the death of King Henry II and a subsequent series of weak kings who could not keep the loyalty of their people. Finally, in 1594, Henry IV became king, gaining the approval of the powerful Catholic League after he converted to Catholicism. In 1598, King Henry ended the Wars of Religion with the Edict of Nantes, which made Protestantism legal in France again, although Catholicism was still the official religion.

France lay in ruins after decades of war, and Henry needed to find ways of rebuilding the country and uniting the people. Henry decided one way to do this was to strengthen France's position in the New World. He founded the Canada and Acadia Company, backed by a group of French merchants, and granted it a **trade monopoly** in North America. Aymar de Clarmont de Chaste led the company, and in 1603, he began to work on setting up trade relations with the First Nations people.

De Chaste died later the same year, and Pierre du Gua de Monts took charge of the company. De Monts concluded the best way to trade with the Native people in Canada was to found a permanent settlement in the New World to serve as a trade outpost.

De Monts' first attempt at colonization, on St. Croix Island in 1604, ended badly. After a terrible winter in which nearly half the colonists died, de Monts sailed south, looking for a better location. Some of the dead had been buried on St. Croix Island, but the island was too small for all the graves; de Monts needed to find a place to bury the rest of his men.

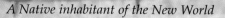
A Native inhabitant of the New World

The French stopped at present-day Cape Cod, but the Native Americans in the area did not want any strangers on their land. Hurriedly, de Monts and his men buried their dead companions, marking their graves with wooden crosses. As soon as they had left the shore, the Native people came out of the nearby woods, pulled up the crosses and threw them into the ocean, and dug up the bodies.

Henry IV of France

Who Were the Huguenots?

Huguenots were Protestants in the highly Catholic France of the sixteenth and seventeenth centuries. They followed John Calvin's beliefs, which were against the Catholic Church's priesthood, sacraments, worship practices, and doctrines. To the Huguenots, salvation was an act of God, just as creation was an act of God. They also believed that they were part of a select group of people—the elect—who had been predestined for salvation.

The Huguenots believed that the Catholic Church's practices could not help someone achieve salvation. Instead, to the Huguenots, it was necessary to live a strict and godly life, not perform rituals, in gratitude for God's salvation.

The French Huguenots became very vocal in their beliefs—and in their opposition to the Roman Catholic faith. They suffered many years of persecution for their beliefs. Among their persecutors was the Catholic League, also known as the Holy League. The aim of this organization was the suppression of Protestantism and its political influence. After Henry III was able to take back some of the concessions he made to the Huguenots, he dissolved the Catholic League. But, when it became apparent that a Protestant would be next in line for the French throne, the organization was re-formed. It gained in power, controlling most of France's large cities, including Paris. Eventually it broke into two groups and was severely weakened. By 1598, the Catholic League was history.

Port Royal

Pierre de Monts sailed away from Cape Cod, horrified at the *desecration* of his companions' graves. Back he went to the north, this time to the east side of the Bay of Fundy, along the west coast of Nova Scotia. Here, he founded a little colony he named Port Royal.

Leaving one of his companions, Samuel de Champlain, in charge of the settlement, de Monts returned to France to raise more funds to support the Canada and Acadia Company. He sent back ships filled with

The Unofficial First Settlement

In 1599, King Henry IV made François Gravé du Pont (usually called Dupont-Gravé) and Pierre Chauvin de Tonnetuit both lieutenant generals of New France. In 1600, the two men set out for New France with four ships and founded a colony at Tadoussac, just inside the mouth of the St. Lawrence River. Dupont-Gravé and Tonnetuit were both Huguenots, though, and the Catholic Church had decreed that no Protestants or Jews would be allowed into New France. Because of this, the Catholic Church refused to acknowledge the colony actually existed. At any rate, the colony did not last long. Dupont-Gravé and Tonnetuit left Canada with a load of furs before winter set in; when they returned in the spring, they discovered only five colonists. Most of the settlers had died, and some had left to live with nearby First Nations people. The remaining colonists went back to France with Dupont-Gravé and Tonnetuit.

Early settlers in New France

supplies and more colonists, under the command of his friend Baron Jean de Biencourt de Poutrincourt.

The first winter in Port Royal was much milder than the previous year on St. Croix Island, but twelve of the forty-five men in the colony still died of scurvy. The next year, 1606, Champlain invented L'Ordre de Bon Temps—the Order of Good Cheer—to counteract the depression the men faced

Desecration *is an insult or damage against something considered holy.*

27

during the long, hard winter. The colonists took turns fixing huge feasts, entertaining each other and the local Mi'kmaq throughout the snowy months. The colonists even put on the first production of a play in the New World, called the Theatre of Neptune in New France.

While Champlain and the Port Royal colonists focused on keeping themselves warm and alive through the winters, de Monts in France had other problems. The merchants who had invested money in the Canada and Acadia Company did not like the direction de Monts was taking the company. They thought he should focus more on obtaining furs than on founding colonies. They saw how the Spanish had gotten rich from their South American colonies, and the merchants wondered what de Monts had done wrong. Finally, the merchants had had enough of de Monts and his Acadian

colony's lack of profits; they cancelled the trade monopoly and left de Monts with no money to fund a company.

When the Port Royal settlers heard the news in 1607, most of them, including Champlain, left North America and sailed back to France. Poutrincourt stayed behind, among the now mostly empty little houses and gardens, maintaining a French presence in the New World.

Québec City

Pierre de Monts had not given up on his dream of founding colonies in Canada to serve as fur trading posts. He persuaded different merchants to fund him and started the de Monts Trading Company. The king granted the new company the trading monopoly previously held by the Canada and Acadia Company. De Monts decided to stay in France this time and oversee the business from there. He sent Champlain to the New World to plant the new colony, naming him lieutenant governor of New France.

Although the Port Royal colony had flourished in a way, keeping up good relations with the nearby Mi'kmaq tribe and planting fields and gardens, the location had made it difficult for de Monts to enforce his monopoly trading rights in Acadia. Champlain and de Monts agreed the new colony should be planted further inland, along the St. Lawrence River, in the area Jacques Cartier

Harvesting wood in the new colony

Hunters in New France

had named Canada. Here, furs could be shipped down the long river, which would be fairly easy to patrol compared to the Acadian coastline.

Champlain arrived in Canada on June 3, 1608, sailed up the St. Lawrence, and chose a spot for the new colony. Less than a century before, the peaceful Iroquoian village of Stadacona had been located there. Since Cartier's visits to the area, the settlement had disappeared, possibly wiped out in epidemics brought by European visitors.

Over the summer and fall, the French worked on laying out the new habitation, or settlement—which Champlain named Québec after the Algonquian word *Kebec*, meaning "the place where the river narrows"—building the store-houses, living quarters, and a wooden *palisade* to go around the colony. However, the Spanish and Basque who fished and traded further down the St. Lawrence at Tadoussac did not like the idea of the French controlling access to the river and imposing their trade monopoly.

*A **palisade** is a fence made of poles driven into the ground.*

Conspirators *are members of a group planning to commit an illegal act.*

One day in September, after the settlement had taken shape, a captain of one of the French ships nervously approached Champlain. Curious, Champlain followed the man a little way into the nearby woods, out of earshot of the colony. Antoine Natel, one of the colony's locksmiths, the captain whispered, had been paid by the Spanish and Basque to kill Champlain. Natel had had second thoughts and wanted to tell Champlain everything, but he was afraid. The captain knew of four other *conspirators*, but he did not know their names.

Three Rivers, one of the growing French towns in the New World

Champlain stalked back into the colony and called Natel into his quarters. Shaking with fear, Natel told Champlain the whole story. The Spanish and Basque had promised to pay the conspirators a lot of money to kill Champlain and turn the new colony over to them. Jean Duval, another locksmith, led the conspiracy.

After a trial, in which all the conspirators were found guilty, Duval was hanged and his head put on a spike on the top of the colony palisade as a warning to anyone who might try to oppose Champlain. Natel was pardoned because of his help in exposing the conspiracy, but Champlain sent the remaining three men back to France where Pierre de Monts would decide what to do with them.

Before winter set in, Champlain sent most of the men back to France. Champlain and twenty-seven other men would stay in Québec. He had experienced three winters in New France, one of them the devastating winter at St. Croix Island, and he thought he knew what to expect.

Champlain probably expected some of his companions to die of scurvy that winter, but he probably did not think he would lose so many of them. Scurvy was a dreadful disease, and no one at that time knew what caused it. Over seventy years before, Jacques Cartier and his suffering companions had been given white cedar tea as a cure for scurvy, but unfortunately Cartier had not written the details of the cure in his journals. By April, only eight of the twenty-eight colonists in Québec survived.

More ships would soon arrive, carrying hundreds of new colonists to Canada. With the founding of Québec, the French had at last established a permanent presence in the New World. For nearly a century France had laid claim to most of the northern half of the east coast of North America, but this claim meant very little without a physical presence in the area. Finally, with the help of men like Pierre de Monts and Samuel de Champlain, that presence was beginning to take root.

An early map of "New France"

Three
THE PROVINCE OF CANADA

As the first light of dawn sparkled on the waters of the lake, the two hundred Mohawk warriors attacked. Samuel de Champlain stood with his two French companions and the mixed group of sixty Montagnais, Algonquin, and Wendat who had accompanied him. As they had sat around their campfires the night before, listening to the two sides screaming insults back and forth at each other, some of the Native men had instructed Champlain on how to recognize the enemy chiefs. Now, Champlain picked out the three Mohawk chiefs, with their elaborate feather headdresses. He raised his musket and quickly shot two of the chiefs, to the shock and alarm of the Mohawks, who had never seen firearms. One of the other Frenchmen killed the third chief, and the rest of the Mohawks fled.

First Alliances

As soon as he put ashore on the banks of the St. Lawrence River, Champlain had made contact with the local Montagnais to work on setting up a fur trading relationship with them. The Montagnais and the Algonquin, their allies, watched as Champlain dealt with the assassination conspiracy. They saw how he moved against the traitors, beheading their leader and putting his head on the wall for all to see. This, they thought, could

*A **confederacy** is an alliance of people, states, or parties for some common purpose.*

be the man to help them in their wars against the Iroquois **Confederacy** south of the Great Lakes.

In the spring of 1609, the chiefs of the Montagnais and Algonquin tribes arrived in Québec to see Champlain, bringing with them a Wendat chief from further upriver. The chiefs wanted Champlain to go with them on a raid against their sworn enemies the Mohawks, the easternmost tribe in the Iroquois Confederacy. Champlain agreed. He thought making an alliance with the local First Nations tribes would be the best way to get their help with fur trading and exploration.

Samuel de Champlain

Alliances with First Nations helped New France colonies grow.

Meanwhile, the English . . .

As the French struggled to colonize Canada and set up a successful fur trade, the English were busy claiming other parts of North America. In 1610, John Guy arrived on the coast of Newfoundland, sent by the English king James I to found a colony. Ever since John Cabot had landed in the Atlantic Provinces in 1497, European fishermen had been traveling across the Atlantic Ocean to fish the cod-rich Grand Banks, southeast of Newfoundland. These fishermen sheltered in Newfoundland's harbors and took in fresh water from the island's abundant streams, but they established no permanent settlements. John Guy's colony at Cuper's Cove was the first official English settlement in Canada. The little colony struggled through the long winters, losing a few people to cold and illness each year, and worked to provide for themselves, despite the fact none of their crops would grow in the thin, rocky soil. In 1614, John Guy gave up and went back to England, although the colony survived until at least 1621, when its governor moved to New England. Many of the colonists did not leave Newfoundland when the colony disbanded, choosing instead to move elsewhere along Newfoundland's coast and start their own settlements. Today, the community of Cupids is located on the site of Guy's colony.

Champlain traveled with the warriors further inland along the St. Lawrence and then south along another river, until they reached a large lake, which Champlain named after himself. At the south end of the lake, near where Ticonderoga, New York, is located today, they finally encountered a Mohawk encampment. The encounter that followed ended with the three Mohawk chiefs lying dead from gunshot wounds—pierced through their wooden armor—a terrifying sight for the Mohawks.

This clash between the northern tribes and the Iroquois Confederacy gave the northern alliance a competitive edge in the conflict, at least for a while. The French had made a powerful enemy in the Iroquois Confederacy, however, an enemy they would have to face for nearly a century.

The Iroquois quickly learned how to survive the guns of the French. Their wooden armor—perfectly capable of stopping the arrows of their First Nations enemies—could not withstand bullets, so the Mohawk war-

"Huron" and "Wendat"

When French explorers came upon the indigenous people living between Lake Simcoe and Lake Huron in what is now Ontario, they called them "Huron." To the new settlers, the men of the Native population wore their hair in a style that reminded them of wild boar, *hure* in French.

The Huron called themselves the Wendat, "people who live on the back of a great turtle." They saw the turtle's back as an island supporting the entire world.

Eventually the Wendat were forced to leave their land. Afterward, some tribal members referred to themselves as the Wyandot, floating islanders. They had lost their home.

riors gave up wearing their armor and started dropping flat on the ground as soon as they saw the French start to fire; the bullets whizzed harmlessly over their heads. The warriors abandoned *formation attacks* as well, becoming skilled at stealth, attacking suddenly while the French reloaded their weapons and then vanishing quickly and silently back into the woods.

Although they changed their fighting techniques in response to the threat of French firearms, the Mohawk wanted their own "fire sticks." Within several years, Dutch traders traveling up the Hudson River and eager to make a good profit would willingly begin selling guns to the Iroquois Confederacy. With the help of firearms, the wars between the Mohawk of the Iroquois Confederacy and the Northern Alliance of Montagnais, Algonquin, Wendat, and French would again be evenly matched.

Formation attacks are battles where the troops fight in a formal shape or structure.

Canoes were vital to the Wendat culture.

Champlain Goes to Wendake

Since his arrival in Québec, Champlain had traded with the Montagnais almost exclusively, exchanging bolts of cloth, woolen blankets, and metal pots for pelts of fur. The Montagnais got most of the furs from the Wendat, a confederacy of First Nations further up the St. Lawrence River, who in turn had received many of the furs in trade from other nations to the north and west. Champlain had met members of the Wendat Confederacy and had sent men as *truchements*—ambassadors—to live in Wendake, the sprawling Wendat territory located in what is now southern Ontario, but he wanted to visit the area himself. The Montagnais tried to discourage Champlain from leaving on the trip—they wanted to keep their privileged position of trade middlemen with the French—but in 1615, after

French trappers intermarried with First Nations people to form a unique culture of skilled woodsmen and navigators.

returning from a trip to France, Champlain went anyway.

In Wendake—which the French called Huronia, just as they called the Wendat Hurons—Champlain set up a direct trade relationship, bypassing the Montagnais as that nation had feared. In return, he agreed to accompany a group of Wendat warriors on a raid against an Iroquois village. The Wendat expected Champlain and his French companions to easily defeat the Iroquois. They had heard about the power of the French guns, and several Wendats had been at Lake Champlain in 1609 to witness the attack against the Mohawk.

Instead of the anticipated triumph, however, the assault against the Iroquois failed; the reinforcements Champlain expected from another nearby tribe did not arrive, and Champlain himself was shot in the knee with an arrow. The Wendat retreated, carrying the wounded Champlain away in a basket.

The Iroquois Confederacy gained new confidence after this encounter. Clearly, the French were not invulnerable.

The Wendat were slightly disappointed their new allies had not lived up to their reputation. They kept up their trade agreement, though, and Champlain spent the winter in Wendake recovering from his knee injury.

Récollet priests, contemplative and strictly observant friars, were part of the Franciscan order.

Black Robes

With the colony of Québec beginning to grow and flourish, the Catholic Church in France decided the time had come to send missionaries to New France to teach the First Nations people about Christianity. On the one hand, they thought converting the Native people would improve trade relations, but on the other hand, they also truly believed the First Nations people needed to learn about God. In 1615, when Champlain returned to Canada from a visit to France, he took with him four *Récollet priests*.

The Récollets moved to Wendake and lived among the people there, studying the Wendat language and teaching the

The Coureurs de Bois

To make doing business with the First Nations peoples easier, Champlain chose a number of young men and sent them to live with the local tribes as *truchements*, or ambassadors. These men learned the Native languages, married Native women, and learned to navigate the Canadian wilderness as though they had been born there. They became known as *coureurs de bois*—woods-runners. They served as guides and translators, acting as go-betweens in French–First Nations interactions. Later, the term referred to any unlicensed trapper. Part heroic figures, part renegade outlaws, coureurs de bois remained an important element of Canadian society for decades.

One of the Jesuit priests who came to New France

Many of the French fur trappers living at Québec and along the river were also unhappy with the presence of the Récollets. Many of these trappers were Huguenots, French Protestants whose families had suffered at the hands of the Roman Catholics during the religious wars of the previous century. They thought the Roman Catholic version of Christianity was wrong, and they disliked the priests teaching their beliefs to the Wendat.

The handful of Récollet priests working in Wendake felt overwhelmed with the job they had been given. Several of them worked on writing descriptions of the Wendat people, their land, and their customs, but none of them had made much progress converting the Wendat to Christianity. Still, they believed the mission was worthwhile. They asked Champlain to send for help from the Jesuits.

The Jesuits were a society of missionary priests who had sent men to Asia, Africa, and South America to preach to the people there. Well organized and very dedicated, the Jesuits had a reputation for success. In 1625, three Jesuit missionaries arrived in Canada to continue the job the Récollets had started.

Unlike the Récollets, the Jesuits did not try to change the culture of the Wendat— their clothing and language—only their

people about God. To truly succeed, however, they thought they needed to make the Wendat more "European" by teaching them French and getting them to wear European clothing.

The Wendat called the priests Black Robes, because they wore long black robes. They resisted the priests' efforts. The Wendat had their own religious beliefs and felt no need to switch to Christianity. Neither did they want to become European.

The modern community of Sainte-Marie among the Hurons re-creates the long-ago lifestyle of their ancestors.

Ville-Marie

When people in France read the writings sent by Jesuit priests in Wendake, many started getting excited about moving to Canada and "converting the savages." One group, called the Mystics, arrived in 1641, led and financed by Jérôme le Royer de la Dauversière and his wife. Le Royer and the volunteers who accompanied him wanted to build a Christian community in Canada. The Jesuits did not like the idea, and the governor of New France called it a "foolhardy enterprise." Nevertheless, in 1642, the little group set up a colony, named Ville-Marie, on an island in the St. Lawrence upriver from Québec (on the former site of the Iroquoian village Hochelaga). Although the Mystics did not succeed in building their ideal community, the colony remained and was later renamed Montréal.

beliefs. For a long time, though, they had no success at all. Still, the Jesuits persevered, learning the Wendat language and winning the respect of some of the Wendats. Father Jean de Brébeuf, one of these men, wrote the first Wendat dictionary and grammar book, along with detailed observations about Wendat culture.

When the Jesuits finally started winning converts among the Wendat, they could not tell who truly believed in Christianity and who were looking for the material advantages conversion could bring them. At around the same time, the French began offering incentives to Native people who became Christians: Christian Natives could buy guns and got better deals in trade negotiations.

The Fall of Wendake

The Jesuits intended to impact Wendat society, but their influence, although huge, was

Shamans *are spiritual leaders.*

A Récollet priest is credited with being the first European to see Niagara Falls.

not what they intended. They meant to transform Wendake into a Christian nation; instead, their presence led to the downfall of the Wendat. When some Wendats began to accept Christianity—either because they believed its message or because they wanted the benefits it would bring in trade—the Jesuits convinced them they needed to abandon the religious practices of their tribe. Other Wendats considered the converts traitors, and tensions rose.

As serious as the divisions caused by the conversions were, more destructive were the epidemics. European diseases unknowingly introduced by priests and French fur traders spread swiftly throughout Wendake. Whole villages died in epidemic after epidemic—measles, influenza, smallpox. By the 1640s, half the population of Wendake had been wiped out, leaving the once-powerful group of nations unable to defend themselves from the attacks of their enemy, the southern Iroquois Confederacy.

Wendat society fell into chaos. Many, encouraged by the *shamans*, blamed the Jesuit priests, whom they now considered evil wizards, saying they cast spells to bring the deadly diseases. Some, feeling their own religion had let them down, rushed to convert to Christianity, hoping that might keep them alive. Others converted after their Christian family members died, since the priests told them only Christians went to heaven and families feared being separated in the afterlife.

Seeing the state of Wendake, the Iroquois pressed their advantage. In 1648, they began a series of raids, massacring thousands and enslaving hundreds more. Seven Jesuit priests, including Father Brébeuf, were captured and tortured to death. In 1649, the survivors—only three hundred Wendats and a handful of French—trickled into Québec. A few had

The martyrdom of Father Brébeuf

fled west. Some still survived with the Iroquois. But the great nation of Wendake was gone, unable to withstand the disease and divisions brought by the French.

From the first terrible winters in St. Croix, Port Royal, and Québec, New France had grown into an established society filled with hundreds of settlers. In the process, the settlers had become involved in a war with the southern Iroquois Confederacy, and their presence had unintentionally caused the end of the great Wendake. The next decades would bring further growth, but it would also bring further war.

To the east, the French province of Acadia had also taken root, growing out of the little colony of Port Royal, founded years earlier in 1605, into a scattering of tiny trading posts along the coasts.

47

Settlers to Acadia would have seen the area's rocky coasts.

Four

ACADIA

Jean de Poutrincourt leaned forward in the boat, looking eagerly toward shore for the buildings of Port Royal. What would be the condition of the little settlement? Ever since he had returned to France two years before, the colony had been abandoned, left to the mercy of winter storms and wild animals. Poutrincourt thought about the repairs he and his men would have to do. Their first task would be finding a suitable place to spend the night.

Poutrincourt jumped out of the boat as it scraped up onto the beach and helped pull it ashore. The Frenchmen lifted out the bundles of supplies they had brought with them from their ship, anchored out in deeper water, and headed up the path toward the deserted colony.

The familiar structures looked exactly as he remembered them, Poutrincourt thought, as he stepped between the buildings into the central courtyard. The stones of the courtyard were neat, without the drifts of dead leaves he had expected.

From across the courtyard he caught a movement out of the corner of his eye. He turned and saw the great Mi'kmaq chief Membertou striding toward him with his arms held out in welcome.

"My friend!" the old chief exclaimed. "You have returned!"

Trade alliances *are coopera-tive agreements regarding trade between two or more groups.*

The French Return to Acadia

Poutrincourt had not wanted to leave Port Royal in 1608, but de Monts had lost his monopoly the year before, which meant anyone who remained behind in Acadia did so illegally. Poutrincourt had given up and returned to France to try and persuade the king to grant him a new monopoly. His efforts had taken nearly two years, but finally King Henry IV had agreed to give Poutrincourt the trading monopoly for the Acadian region. Poutrincourt had been able to find a group of merchants to support the expedition.

Poutrincourt arrived back in Port Royal in June 1610, expecting to find the buildings in need of repairs and the colony looking rundown and shabby. Instead, he discovered the local Mi'kmaq tribe had looked after the settlement, and the French

Modern reconstruction of the settlement at Port Royal

were able to quickly take up residence in Port Royal again.

The Mi'kmaq and the French

In some parts of North America, European settlers lived in fear of brutal attacks from nearby Native tribes. Even in Québec, where Samuel de Champlain had organized *trade alliances* with the Montagnais and Wendat, the First Nations people did not always trust their French allies. In Acadia, however, the French enjoyed a close relationship with the local Mi'kmaq tribes.

From the time of the earliest French explorers, the Mi'kmaq had been open and friendly, willing to trade furs for European goods and to help the newcomers out in any way they needed. Membertou, grand chief over the Mi'kmaq nation, led the way in establishing a good relationship with the newcomers.

Membertou, if the French correctly understood his stories of personally meeting Jacques Cartier seventy years before, was over a hundred years old by the time the colony of Port Royal was founded in 1605. Despite his apparent great age, he looked only about fifty years old, wrote Marc Lescarbot, who spent a winter in Port Royal.

During the first winter after Poutrincourt's return to Port Royal, no settlers died, a rare thing in those days. The likeliest explanation for this was that the French had

Jesuits in Acadia

In 1611, two Jesuit missionaries, Pierre Biard and Énemond Massé, arrived in Port Royal, followed the next year by Father Gilbert du Thet, much to the annoyance of Poutrincourt's nineteen-year-old son Biencourt. Poutrincourt's family had originally been Huguenots, but pressures from France had caused them to switch to Catholicism; Huguenots were not officially allowed into New France. The Jesuits did not live in Port Royal, however, choosing instead to stay with the nearby Mi'kmaq.

In 1613, the Jesuits moved to Mount Desert Island, in what is now Maine, to set up their own colony. Unfortunately, they arrived only a month before the English captain Samuel Argall began his attacks on French Acadia.

The Jesuit priests Biard, Massé, and du Thet, although they did not stay long, were the first Jesuits in New France. They arrived fourteen years before their fellow Jesuits reached Québec to preach to the Wendat.

the help of the Mi'kmaq, who knew how to avoid or cure diseases like scurvy.

On June 24, 1610, shortly after Poutrincourt's return to Acadia, Grand Chief Membertou became the first of the Mi'kmaq people to accept baptism as a Catholic; many more soon followed his lead. With his baptism, Membertou took the Christian name Henry, after France's King Henry IV who had died two months before.

Chief Membertou died in Port Royal on September 18, 1611. As he lay dying, he spoke to his relatives, telling them to make sure the Mi'kmaq continued their friendship with the French after he died. He was buried in the French graveyard at Port Royal, at a funeral attended by all the French and many Mi'kmaq.

Trouble Brewing

Life in Acadia was turbulent for the settlers over the next several decades. In 1613, the English attacked Port Royal and occupied Acadia until the Treaty of St. Germain-en-Laye in 1632 returned control of the province to France.

Cardinal Richelieu, the young King Louis XIII's chief minister, appointed his cousin Isaac de Razilly as governor of the newly re-claimed province. In Acadia, de Razilly made friends with Charles La Tour, who had lived in Acadia since he was a teenager, ar-riving with his father and Jean de Poutrincourt in 1610. La Tour had married a Mi'kmaq woman and had several children with her before her early death. He had lived in the Acadian woods as a fur trader.

La Tour and de Razilly worked out an agreement—de Razilly and his men would control the fur trade from La Hève, on the southeast coast of what is now Nova Scotia, and La Tour would take the area around the Bay of Fundy. This agreement worked well, but in 1635, de Razilly died and was re-placed the next year by his cousin Charles de Menou d'Aulnay.

Cardinal Richelieu

D'Aulnay had no patience with La Tour, whom he considered a backwoods peasant. D'Aulnay had rich and powerful friends and was well known in the royal court of France. He wanted to control the entire

Acadia's winters were long and cold.

Acadian fur trade, and he wanted La Tour out. For a few years he tried, with the help of his friends in France, to convince King Louis XIII to take away La Tour's lands and give them to him, but the king supported La Tour's claim.

Civil War Breaks Out

By 1640, D'Aulnay had gotten tired of trying to get rid of La Tour legally. When La Tour— who had been in France marrying his second wife, Françoise Jacquelin—sailed into the Bay of Fundy and headed for Port Royal, he discovered his way blocked by d'Aulnay's ships. After an exchange of gunfire, La Tour left and sailed across the bay to Fort La Tour, near the mouth of the St. John River.

For the next five years, the two men would be at war, raiding each other's settlements and attacking each other's ships. La Tour, the weaker party, made frequent trips

south to the English colonies around Boston to buy supplies and gather support.

Early in 1645, while La Tour was away on one of these trips, d'Aulnay attacked Fort La Tour directly. La Tour's wife, Françoise, defended the fort with her husband's men, even leading a hand-to-hand combat attack when d'Aulnay broke through the defenses into the fort itself.

Françoise was badly outnumbered by d'Aulnay's men, and the defenders had almost run out of ammunition. To save the lives of the defending soldiers, she agreed to surrender the fort to d'Aulnay. As soon as he had taken them prisoner, though, d'Aulnay went back on his promise to Françoise and hanged all La Tour's men. Françoise herself died a few days later in d'Aulnay's prison, some say of a broken heart, some say of poison.

For the next five years d'Aulnay ruled Acadia as governor, and La Tour was not able to return. Then, in 1650, while traveling along the coast, d'Aulnay's canoe capsized,

*Acadia's serene landscape does
not match its history.*

spilling him into icy waters. D'Aulnay dragged himself to shore, but he was soaked through and very cold. He died of cold and exposure before he was able to get back to his camp.

As soon as d'Aulnay was dead, La Tour came back to Acadia. Some must have thought the war would start all over again, since d'Aulnay had left a widow and men loyal to him. Instead, La Tour married Jeanne Motin, d'Aulnay's widow, uniting the control of Acadia in one house.

The history of Acadia, named for the simple, peaceful Arcadia of Ancient Greece, was neither simple nor peaceful. Early on, the settlers faced terrible winters and deaths from scurvy. Later, they had to deal with attacks by the English and then with an ongoing feud between two men who both wanted to govern them. The most positive aspect of early Acadian history seems to be the Mi'kmaq, who openly befriended the French, teaching them how to survive the winters and accepting their presence without hostility.

The Acadian colonists had faced many challenges by 1650, but the next hundred years would be even more difficult. The English would not give up until they had claimed the land for their own.

While Acadia remained a sparsely populated handful of trading outposts, the province of Canada, along the St. Lawrence River, had begun to grow. Help from the king of France would soon transform it into a thriving colony.

The arrival of the filles du roi

Five

THE ROYAL PROVINCE

The ship bumped against the side of the dock, signaling the end of the long journey. But in a way, thought Marie-Claude Chamois, looking over the railing at the small group of people gathered to greet the ship, this was only the beginning. She was fourteen years old, and she had come to Québec, along with over a hundred other girls, to provide wives for the men of New France. They were the *filles du roi*.

The journey from France had taken nearly three months, and conditions on the ship had been terrible. Many girls had been sick for almost the entire voyage, which did not improve the atmosphere on board.

For the last three months, Marie-Claude had thought about her future, wondering if she had done the right thing in leaving her homeland, wondering about the unknown man she would marry. She looked at the knot of rough-hewn men standing on the dock and wondered if one of them would be her husband.

King Louis Takes Charge

In 1661, King Louis XIV's chief minister died, and instead of replacing him, the twenty-two-year-old king decided to take charge of his kingdom himself. Louis XIV had been king since he was four years old, but his mother and his chief ministers had made all the decisions for him until he was old enough to rule on his own.

As the young king looked at the state of his kingdom, he noticed things were not going well in New France, in the settlements of Canada along the St. Lawrence River. Although the colony had been in existence for over fifty years, the population was only about 3,000 and had stopped growing. In comparison, the North American colonies of their rivals the English, founded at the same time or later, had grown to over 100,000 people.

For the last thirty-five years, the Company of One Hundred Associates, a group originally headed by Cardinal Richelieu, had run Canada. The purpose of the company was to recruit settlers to go to New France and convert the First Nations people of Canada—and to make a profit, of course. The company had accomplished none of these goals, however, and the colony was a mess. Iroquois attacks on settlers had increased, and as a result, few people in France wanted to risk their lives in Canada.

King Louis decided to disband the Company of One Hundred Associates and to take over the running of his colony himself. On September 24, 1663, he signed a decree making New France a royal province. This meant he and his appointees would now make the decisions concerning New France, rather than leave the colony in the hands of a group of investors.

Canada already had a governor, but King Louis thought the colony needed something

Louis XIV

more. In 1665, he sent Jean Talon to Québec to serve as an intendant, a royal administrator whose job it was to make sure the colony made more money. Technically, the intendant was subject to the governor, but in reality he had farther-reaching power than the governor.

Jean Talon leapt into his job with enthusiasm. He had dozens of ideas for improving life in the colony. He built a shipyard, imported looms so the colonists could make their own cloth, brought over horses from Europe, and started a brewery (which failed). Talon wanted the settlers to be able to live independently from France.

Daughters of the King

One of the first things Jean Talon did after arriving in Québec was to conduct a census.

Women did their part in building New France.

He wanted to figure out why the colony was not growing as it should. He discovered there were very few eligible single women compared to the number of single men.

Talon came up with the brilliant idea of importing young women to fill the gender gap and provide wives for the many unmarried men. The nearly one thousand young French women who would arrive over the next ten years were known as the *filles du roi*, "daughters of the king." They arrived by the shipload, were quickly taken under the care of nuns, and were almost immediately married off to the young men of New France.

The system worked surprisingly well, especially after Talon threatened the young men who did not want to give up their bachelor lifestyle with the loss of their hunting and trading rights if they did not quickly marry. The qualifications for the girls were that they be unmarried, healthy, pretty, and of good moral character. Talon also requested country girls, since he thought they would be more used to hard work and better able to adjust to colony life. Some critics of the scheme claimed France sent over women from their prisons to get rid of them and that Québec had become nothing more than a bawdy **penal colony**. Talon and the settlers hotly denied these charges. If they discovered a girl had lived an immoral life in France, the governor of New France stated, they sent her back immediately.

The king gave each girl a chest of items such as handkerchiefs, needles, and combs to take with her for her new life. He also arranged for the men to be paid at the time of their marriage. To encourage the settlers to have large families, Talon set up a system in which each family was paid yearly depending on the number of children they had—the more living children in a family, the more money the parents received.

Marie-Claude Chamois, the fourteen-year-old girl who arrived from France in 1670, married François Frigon and had seven children. Some filles du roi had as many as eighteen or twenty children. Talon's idea had solved the population problem in

Canada; by 1672, six years after the census, the population had more than doubled to 6,700.

Landlords of Québec

Years before Jean Talon had arrived in New France to serve as intendant, Cardinal Richelieu had started up the seigneurial system to increase the number of settlers. Under the system, the *seigneurs*—landlords—would be granted land with the understanding they would bring over workers from France

A *penal colony* is a place of imprisonment at a remote location.

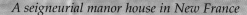

A seigneurial manor house in New France

Feudal lords were power-ful property owners in me-dieval Europe with author-ity over an area, castle, or community.

Aristocrats are members of a country's highest so-cial class.

to live on it and would put money into developing it. Most seigneurs did not even live on their own land, and the system did not help to increase the population to the extent Cardinal Richelieu had hoped.

Talon changed the seigneurial system by making a law stating all seigneurs had to live on their own land. If these men were going to own land in New France, Talon wanted them to truly be a part of the colony.

Many of these landlords worked the land along with their tenants, sharing their labor and hardships. Even though the seigneurs owned the land and the tenants merely leased it from them, this shared work created a bond. Instead of being distant *feudal lords*, many seigneurs did not seem very dif-ferent from the men who worked their land.

Talon also changed the landscape of Québec, although he did not restrict this change to seigneurial land. He encour-

Bishop Laval and the Education of Québec

François Laval, a Jesuit priest, arrived in Québec in 1659, ready to do God's work. Four years later, in 1663, he founded the Séminaire de Québec to train more priests. The sémi-naire was the first college in Canada and years later would become Laval University. In 1678, he built a school to train craftsmen as well. Laval was named the first Bishop of Québec in 1674.

aged the development of "ribbon farms," long, skinny lots stretching back from the river's edge. This style of farms allowed the maximum number of people to have access to the river. It also meant the settlers all lived very close to each other and could help each other easily if anyone had trouble.

Being Canadien

Jean Talon's efforts had paid off. He had arrived in a struggling colony whose population looked as though it might begin decreasing. When he left, six years later, the number of settlers in Québec had risen sharply, and the colony had become self-supporting. The colonists had begun to develop their own national identity; they were starting to become *Canadien*, not just French.

The Canadiens were a rugged people, able to survive and prosper in the rough Canadian wilderness. Few **aristocrats** wanting lives of luxury came to New France, although France had plenty of them. Canada had aristocrats, but they were sometimes hard to tell from the general population. Everyone had to work hard in the New World.

Living so far away from their king did not make the settlers disloyal, but they were much less worried about what he might

Canadien settlers

think of them. Living thousands of miles away, they had no awe of King Louis the Sun King.

French officials visiting Québec noticed the differences between the settlers and the common people of France. "They are too proud," they said and shook their heads. They *were* proud; after all, they had carved a new life for themselves in the wilds of a new land. They were Canadien.

One of the Hudson's Bay Company's forts

Six

WARS AND CONFLICTS IN NEW FRANCE

The light canoes slipped silently through the water of James Bay, heading for the English fort. It was late June 1686, and Pierre de Troyes had traveled with one hundred men north from Montréal for three months to reach their targets—the three English forts of the Hudson's Bay Company. They were exhausted, but the English would never guess that from their ferocity.

The soldiers at the forts did not even see de Troyes arrive. They were completely unprepared for an attack, especially one from the south. To the north lay Hudson Bay, but English ships traveled those waters. The forts might have had warning if the French had arrived in warships from that direction.

De Troyes took just over one month to capture the three forts that lay scattered around the south end of James Bay. Each battle was fairly short, the first taking only half an hour. The English never knew how worn out and short of supplies the Canadiens were or they might have resisted harder. They didn't realize that de Troyes and his men had no reserves to fall back on.

The Hudson's Bay Company

In 1610, seventy-six years before Pierre de Troyes' raid, the English explorer Henry Hudson had sailed into the icy northern Hudson Bay while searching for the Northwest Passage—the water route through North America to the Pacific Ocean.

Excited about discovering the huge body of water, Hudson was sure he had found what he was looking for. He sailed around the bay until he reached the smaller James Bay at its south end, and there he found he could sail no further south. For months, Hudson and his men explored the area and drew detailed maps, but they stayed too long. By November, their ship was frozen into the ice. After a winter of eating moss to fill their empty bellies, Hudson's men had lost all re-

Henry Hudson's ship

spect for their captain. When the ice thawed, they abandoned Hudson, along with a few others, and went home to England. Nobody ever found out what happened to Henry Hudson; nothing was ever heard about him again.

The English wanted to know if Hudson Bay might actually be the beginning of the Northwest Passage. They continued to explore its coasts but quickly discovered the bay had no outlet to the Pacific Ocean.

In 1659, French explorers and fur traders, Pierre-Esprit Radisson and Médard Chouart des Groseilliers, proposed to the governor of Québec that they travel into the unknown areas to the northwest to look for new sources of fur. The governor thought this would be a good idea, but he wanted them to take two government officials with them. He also wanted to charge them half their profits. Angry, Radisson and Groseilliers left and made the voyage anyhow, on their own. Then, instead of returning to Québec with the information they had discovered, they traveled to England. The two men told the English king Charles II he could use Hudson Bay to access the fur trade. Charles liked the idea; up until now, the French had controlled the entire Canadian supply of furs.

In 1668, Radisson and Groseilliers sailed with the English to Hudson Bay and helped them establish trade relations with the First

The Hudson Bay's icy waters

The French wanted to expand their fur trade north of Lake Ontario.

Nations people—the Cree. In 1670, King Charles granted the Hudson's Bay Company a monopoly on trade for an area comprising over three million square miles (eight million square kilometers). Today, the Hudson's Bay Company is still in existence, one of the oldest companies in the world.

The French did not like the English being in Hudson Bay. Many of their First Nations trading allies had started trading with the English instead of the French, since Hudson Bay was closer to them than the St. Lawrence River. For a while, the French tried sending men north to trade with the Cree before the English got there, but the voyage took months and involved canoeing along a series of rivers, carrying the canoes around rapids and waterfalls. The journey was much too long and difficult to make trading this way practical.

In the 1680s, the French formed the Compagnie du Nord (Company of the North) as a rival to the Hudson's Bay Company. Then, in 1686, they sent Pierre de Troyes and his men north to seize the English trading forts. The mission was successful, and for the next twenty-five years the French would control James Bay and the southern end of Hudson Bay. This takeover created problems with the English and served to also stir up problems with another old enemy—the Iroquois Confederacy.

Troubles with the Iroquois

The French attacks on the James Bay forts did not directly antagonize the Iroquois Confederacy, but both de Troyes' attacks and the growing problems with the Iroquois were related to the French wanting more and more furs. As the French explored further into the Canadian wilderness to the west, they irritated the Iroquois, who had their own fur trading empire. To make matters worse, in 1684 and again in 1687, the

French launched attacks on the Iroquois Confederacy, hoping to drive them away from the north side of Lake Ontario where the French wanted to expand their fur trade.

In August 1689, the Iroquois struck back, attacking the little settlement of Lachine and killing dozens of people. For the next twelve years, the French and Iroquois Wars raged, the bloodiest, most violent conflict North America has ever experienced.

In fact, the French and Iroquois Wars had been going on for nearly fifty years by the time of the Lachine Massacre, but they had mostly consisted of intermittent attacks and raids. In the 1690s, the fighting became much worse and much more intense.

Madeleine Saves the Day

In 1692, fourteen-year-old Madeleine de Verchères heard shots and saw a group of Iroquois warriors running toward her father's fort. The attack at Lachine three years earlier was still on everyone's mind, and Madeleine was determined not to let the same thing happen to her family. Her parents were both away, so Madeleine took charge of her little brothers, slammed shut the gates of the fort, and fired her father's musket over the walls. For a week, Madeleine, along with her twelve-year-old brothers, two soldiers, an old man, and several women and children, defended the fort until the French soldiers arrived, managing to convince the Iroquois the fort was fully manned.

Comte de Frontenac

The fighting with the Iroquois was heating up, and the king of France, Louis XIV, needed someone who could take care of the problem. In 1689, he reappointed Louis de Buade, Comte de Frontenac, as governor of New France. Frontenac had served as governor from 1672 to 1682, but had lost his position because he could not get along with the other government officials in the colony. Now, New France needed Frontenac, a man who would go as far as necessary—or farther—to deal with the Iroquois Confederacy.

Frontenac at first tried to negotiate with the Iroquois, but when that did not work, he launched terrible, violent attacks on Iroquois settlements. Frontenac also saw beyond the Iroquois to the English. For centuries, the English and French had never really gotten along, and the English were still upset about the loss of their trading forts in James Bay and Hudson Bay. Instead of attacking the French outright, the English supplied the Iroquois Confederacy with guns and ammunition and encouraged them to keep attacking the French settlements along the St. Lawrence.

In February 1690, Frontenac gathered a group of French soldiers and First Nations warriors and sent them south to Schenectady and two other English colonies, in

Old Québec City early in its history

Phips before the seige of Québec

William Phips

what is now New York State. The attacks were ruthless and brutal. Frontenac's forces slaughtered men, women, and children, leaving the survivors terrified and wanting revenge.

That fall, English warships sailed up the St. Lawrence River, commanded by William Phips. Phips laid siege to Québec and demanded Frontenac's surrender. In response, Frontenac fired his cannons at the English ships. Phips did not stay long in Québec; winter was near, and he worried his ships would get trapped in the ice. Also, a number of his men had gotten sick with smallpox, and Frontenac's cannons had damaged their ships badly. Eight days after he had arrived, Phips left and returned to Boston.

d'Iberville Attacks Newfoundland

Not satisfied with attacking the English colonies to the south, Frontenac looked east to Newfoundland. The English-controlled island stood between France and New France and controlled the wealth of the cod fishery. In 1696, Frontenac sent Pierre Le Moyne d'Iberville to launch raids on the English colonies of Newfoundland's southeastern Avalon Peninsula. For nearly a year, d'Iberville stormed up and down the coast, burning settlements and murdering settlers. By the time he left, recalled to launch an attack on the English in Hudson Bay, thirty-six communities had been destroyed, ninety ships sunk, two hundred colonists killed, and another seven hundred colonists taken prisoner. Only the little town of Carbonear had been able to hold out against the French.

In 1697, England and France had signed the Treaty of Ryswick, ending a conflict in Europe. This put an end to France's attacks against Newfoundland for a while, although it did not end all hostilities between the two countries.

d'Iberville

The Great Peace

The Iroquois were tired of fighting. Their population had dwindled, and the costs of war had outweighed its gains. In 1701, New France and the Iroquois Confederacy signed a peace treaty at Montréal, called the *Grande Paix* (Great Peace). The two sides agreed to stop all attacks and raids, and the Iroquois agreed to stay neutral in any future conflicts between the French and English. The French also granted the Iroquois the right to trade within New France.

The terrible French and Iroquois Wars had ended, but the issue that started them originally, the fur trade, had almost stopped being a problem. More settlers had begun farming instead of relying on the fur trade to survive, and Canada still had access to furs from its northern allies.

By the end of the seventeenth century, New France was settled with established colonies.

New France was less than a hundred years old by the end of the seventeenth century but that time had been filled with wars, raids, and tensions with the Canadian First Nations, the Iroquois Confederacy, and the English. The next century would bring even more problems with England as the two nations fought for control of Canada.

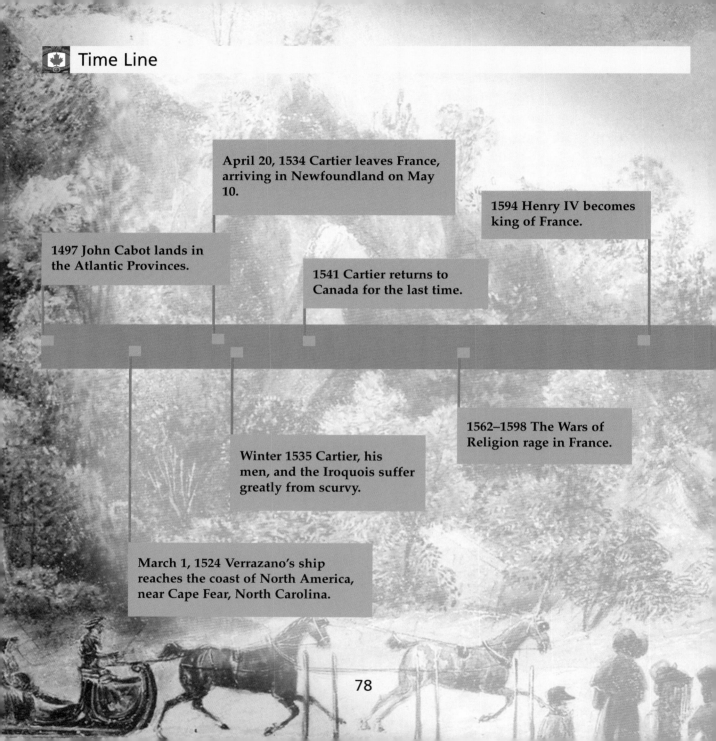

April 20, 1534 Cartier leaves France, arriving in Newfoundland on May 10.

1594 Henry IV becomes king of France.

1497 John Cabot lands in the Atlantic Provinces.

1541 Cartier returns to Canada for the last time.

1562–1598 The Wars of Religion rage in France.

Winter 1535 Cartier, his men, and the Iroquois suffer greatly from scurvy.

March 1, 1524 Verrazano's ship reaches the coast of North America, near Cape Fear, North Carolina.

1606 Champlain invents L'Ordre de Bon Temps—the Order of Good Cheer—to counteract the depression the men faced during the difficult winter; the colonists put on the first production of a play in the New World, called the Theatre of Neptune, in New France.

1604 De Monts makes first attempt at colonization, on St. Croix Island.

June 3, 1608 Champlain arrives in Canada and sails up the St. Lawrence River.

1610 Englishman Henry Hudson sails into Hudson Bay looking for the Northwest Passage.

1607 Most Port Royal settlers, including Champlain, return to France when funding is lost.

1610 Englishman John Guy arrives on the coast of Newfoundland and founds Cuper's Cove, the first official English settlement in Canada.

1605 Colony of Port Royal is founded.

June 24, 1610 Grand Chief Membertou becomes the first Mi'kmaq to be baptized a Catholic.

1620 Pilgrims arrive in America.

1645 d'Aulnay attacks Fort La Tour.

1613 The English attack Port Royal and occupy Acadia until the Treaty of St. Germain-en-Laye in 1632.

1641 The Mystics arrive to build a Christian community in Canada.

1642 The Mystics establish the colony of Ville-Marie.

1625 Three Jesuit missionaries arrive in Canada.

1615 Champlain returns to Canada, bringing with him four Récollet priests.

1663 François Laval, a Jesuit priest, establishes the Séminaire de Québec to train more priests, the first college in Canada.

1661 King Louis XIV takes charge of his kingdom himself.

1697 England and France sign the Treaty of Ryswick, ending a conflict in Europe.

1674 François Laval is named the first Bishop of Québec.

1701 New France and the Iroquois Confederacy sign a peace treaty at Montréal, called the Grande Paix (Great Peace).

September 24, 1663 King Louis XIV signs a decree making New France a royal province.

1678 François Laval builds a school to train craftsmen.

FURTHER READING

Bjornlund, Lydia D. *Iroquois*. Farmington Hills, Mich.: Thomson Gale, 2001.

Coulter, Tony. *Jacques Cartier, Samuel de Champlain, and the Explorers of Canada*. New York: Chelsea House, 1993.

Dunn, Mary R. *Mohawk*. San Diego, Calif.: Lucent Books, 2003.

Graymont, Barbara. *The Iroquois*. New York: Chelsea House, 1988.

Harmon, Daniel E. *Jacques Cartier and the Exploration of Canada*. New York: Chelsea House, 2000.

Libal, Autumn. *Huron*. Philadelphia, Pa.: Mason Crest, 2003.

Rogers, Stillman D. *Montreal*. New York: Scholastic Library, 2000.

Treanor, Nick, ed. *The History of Nations: Canada*. Farmington Hill, Mich.: Thomson Gale, 2003.

Wartik, Nancy. *The French Canadians*. New York: Chelsea House, 1989.

Xydes, Georgia. *Alexander MacKenzie and the Explorers of Canada*. New York: Chelsea House, 1992.

FOR MORE INFORMATION

Canada: A People's History
history.cbc.ca/histicons

Canadian Museum of Civilization,
Jean Talon
www.civilization.ca/educat/oracle/
modules/cgourdeau/page01_e.html

Cartier-Brébeuf National Historic
Site of Canada
www.pc.gc.ca/lhn-nhs/qc/cartierbrebeuf/
index_e.asp

The Cataraqui Archeological Research
Foundation
www.carf.info/kingstonpast/
frenchcataraqui.php

Jesuits in Canada
www.jesuits.ca/history/summary.html

Pathfinders & Passageways:
The Exploration of Canada
www.collectionscanada.ca/explorers/
index-e.html

Port Royal, National Historic
Site of Canada
www.pc.gc.ca/lhn-nhs/ns/portroyal/
index_e.asp

Saint Croix Island International
Historic Site
www.pc.gc.ca/lhn-nhs/nb/stcroix/
index_e.asp

The St. Lawrence: Maritime Seaway and
Economic Centre of Canada, History
collections.ic.gc.ca/stlauren/sl.htm

The Virtual Museum of New France
www.civilization.ca/vmnf/vmnfe.asp

Publisher's note:
The Web sites listed on this page were active at the time of publication. The publisher is not responsible for Web sites that have changed their addresses or discontinued operation since the date of publication. The publisher will review and update the Web-site list upon each reprint.

INDEX

PICTURE CREDITS

Canadian National Parks: pp. 50–51

French National Library: p. 22

National Archives of Canada: pp. 1, 10 (bottom right), 11, 14, 15, 40–41, 72–73, 74 (left), 78–79, 80–81

National Library of Canada: pp. 12, 16–17

National Library of Quebec: p. 36 (left)

Philippe de Champaigne: p. 53

PhotoDisc: p. 39

Photos.com: pp. 18, 48–49, 54–55, 56, 69, 70–71

Sainte-Marie among the Hurons, Midland, Ontario, Canada: p. 44

U.S. Environmental Protection Agency: p. 34

Yale Map Collection: pp. 8, 20

To the best knowledge of the publisher, all other images are in the public domain. If any image has been inadvertently uncredited, please notify Harding House Publishing Service, Vestal, New York 13850, so that rectification can be made for future printings.

BIOGRAPHIES

Sheila Nelson was born in Newfoundland and grew up in both Newfoundland and Ontario. She has written a number of history books for kids and always enjoys the chance to keep learning. She recently earned a master's degree and now lives in Rochester, New York, with her husband and daughter.

SERIES CONSULTANT

Dr. David Bercuson is the Director of the Centre for Military and Strategic Studies at the University of Calgary. His writings on modern Canadian politics, Canadian defense and foreign policy, and Canadian military, among other topics, have appeared in academic and popular publications. Dr. Bercuson is the author, coauthor, or editor of more than thirty books, including *Confrontation at Winnipeg: Labour, Industrial Relations, and the General Strike* (1990), *Colonies: Canada to 1867* (1992), *Maple Leaf Against the Axis, Canada's Second World War* (1995), and *Christmas in Washington: Roosevelt and Churchill Forge the Alliance* (2005). He has also served as historical consultant for several film and television projects, as well as provided political commentary for CBC radio and television and CTV television. In 1989, Dr. Bercuson was elected a fellow of the Royal Society of Canada. In 2004, Dr. Bercuson received the Vimy Award, sponsored by the Conference of Defence Association Institute, in recognition of his significant contributions to Canada's defense and the preservation of the Canadian democratic principles.